And children, like Maui, have time to play.

·R. BURNINGHAM·

Now the sun hurries only half of the year. During the other half he moves slowly across the sky.
Men have time to catch fish.
Farmers have time to plant their crops.
Women have time to dry their tapa.

And each time Maui raised his war club and broke the sun's leg with a mighty whack.

At last the sun called out in a weak voice, "Stop! I will make a deal with you!"

"How do I know that you will keep your promise?" asked Maui.

"You have broken all of my strong legs," said the sun. "I cannot move as fast as I once did."

The sun tried again and again to free himself.
Each time a leg appeared Maui lassoed it and called,
"Promise to cross the sky more slowly. Then I will let
you go."
Each time the sun shouted, "I will not promise!"

So Maui raised his war club high over his head. With a mighty whack he broke the sun's leg.

"I am Maui. The fishermen need more time to catch their fish. The farmers need more time to plant their crops. The women need more time to dry their tapa. I need more time to play. Promise that you will cross the sky more slowly. Then I will let you go."

"I will not promise!" roared the sun.

The sun put up a great struggle. He strained against the rope that held him. He pulled with all his might. He tried again and again to free himself. But Maui held on to the lasso and would not let go.

"Who are you? Why are you doing this to me? Let me go right now!" the sun cried.

The next morning the sun's first leg, or ray, climbed into the crater. Maui whirled his lasso. It whipped out and caught the sun's leg. Quickly Maui pulled the lasso tight.

R. BURNINGHAM.

Up the volcano Maui climbed. He took his lasso and his war club. When he reached the top, he hid in a cave.

·R. BURNINGHAM·

For days Maui watched the sun. He watched it come up in the morning. He watched it climb over the crater of the volcano and hurry across the sky. He watched the darkness come over the land as the sun went to sleep.

"I know what I will do," said Maui, for he had many magical powers.

He made a strong rope and tied it into a lasso.

·R.BURNINGHAM·

Maui passed his mother's house. He heard sad chanting. "What is the matter?" Maui asked his mother.

His mother answered, "We work hard beating the tapa. Then it must dry in the sun. But before it can dry, night comes. The day is so short. Why does the sun cross the sky so quickly? Maui, you must make the sun slow down!"

Maui saw two farmers looking out over the bare fields.
"Why aren't you working?" he asked.

Said one farmer, "We have no time to plant our crops.
Our crops do not have enough sun to grow."

"The day is too short. Why does the sun cross the sky so
quickly?" Maui asked himself.

Maui walked on. He came to a place where sweet potato vines grew. But only a few brown vines still curled around the mounds.

He passed the paddies where taro grew. But only a few yellowed taro leaves floated on the water.

He passed the fields where sugar cane grew. But only a few dried stalks of cane still poked their heads above the ground.

R. BURNINGHAM.

Maui asked himself, "Why is the day so short? Why does the sun cross the sky so quickly?"

Maui peered into the canoe.

"How many fish did you catch?" he asked.

"Not one," answered one of the men.

The other man said, "We know where there are many fish. It is not far from here. But by the time we reach that place the sun is setting. We have to turn around and paddle home."

Maui walked along the beach on his way home. He saw two men. They were pulling their canoe up onto the sand. They did not look very happy.

As the wind played with his kite, Maui looked around. He saw that the sun was going down. He saw shadows all around him.

"Oh, no," he cried. "The day is so short. It is time to go home. Why does the sun cross the sky so quickly?"

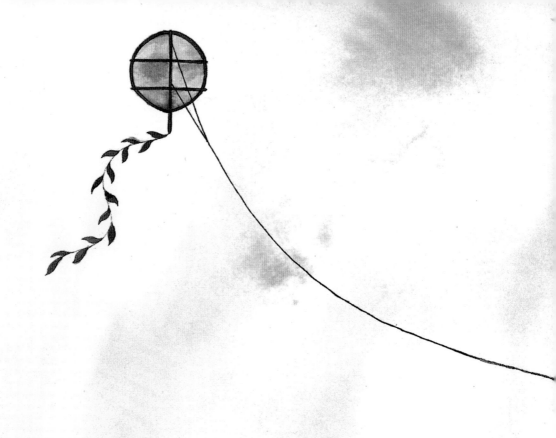

The wind tugged at the kite as it danced in the sky.
Up, up it went. Maui could hardly see it as it darted in and
out of the clouds. He was having such fun!

R BURNINGHAM.

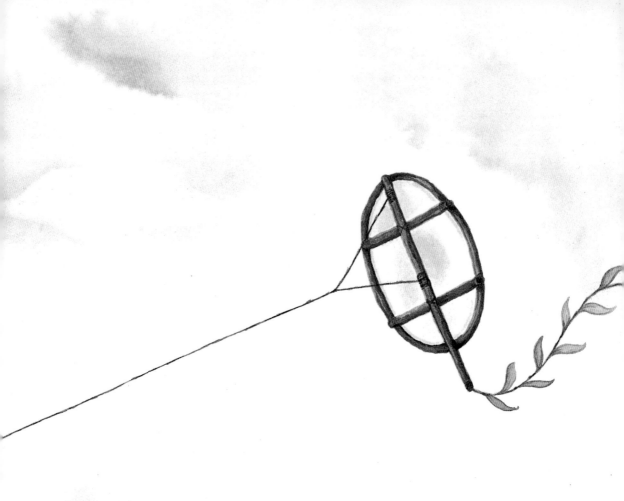

Holding the kite string, he began to run. Faster and faster he went. A gust of wind caught the kite. It soared high into the sky.

Maui looked at all of his kites.
"Today I will fly my biggest one," he thought.
"How high will it go?"

Maui opened his eyes and yawned. He looked out. The sky was clear. A good wind was blowing. What a fine day to fly a kite!

Acknowledgments

How Maui Slowed the Sun is inspired by *Tales of the Menehune,* a collection of Hawaiian legends told to noted storyteller Caroline Curtis by Hawaiian authority Mary Kawena Pukui.

I wish to thank Pat Bova, former children's librarian at Waimanalo Community-School Library, for providing the initial impetus for this book.

I also wish to thank Dr. Donald D. Kilolani Mitchell, consultant in Hawaiian culture at The Kamehameha Schools/Bernice Pauahi Bishop Estate and research associate in anthropology at the Bernice Pauahi Bishop Museum, for reading the manuscript and checking the illustrations for historical accuracy.

S.C.T.

I gratefully acknowledge the love and support of my husband, parents, and children. Their warm encouragement helped in a large way to make the illustrations for this book possible.

R.Y.B.

To
Rick and Jerry
Chip

And to
Hung Leong and Mabel Ching
Irene Tune

07 06 05 04 03 02   9 8 7 6 5 4

Library of Congress Cataloging-in-Publication Data

Tune, Suelyn Ching, 1944–
    How Maui slowed the sun / by Suelyn Ching Tune ; illustrated by
Robin Yoko Burningham.
    p. cm. — (A Kolowalu book)
    Summary: Recounts how Maui uses his magical powers to slow the
path of the sun across the sky, thus allowing crops more time to
grow, fishermen more time to fish, and children more time to play.
    ISBN-13: 978-0–8248-1083–2
    ISBN-10: 0–8248–1083–X
    1. Maui (Polynesian deity)—Juvenile literature. [1. Maui
(Polynesian deity) 2. Folklore—Hawaii.] I. Burningham, Robin
Yoko, ill. II. Title.
PZ8.1.T748Ho 1988
398.2'6'09969—dc19
[E]   88–4548
                                                                        CIP
                                                                          AC

University of Hawai'i Press books are printed on
acid-free paper and meet the guidelines for permanence
and durability of the Council on Library Resources.

How Maui Slowed the Sun

by Suelyn Ching Tune

illustrated by Robin Yoko Burningham

A Kolowalu Book
University of Hawaii Press • Honolulu